All That Glitters

By: Veronica Patrice

PaperCut

Publishing Inc.

This book is a work of fiction. Except for passing reference to real celebrities, all characters are entirely imagined and any resemblance to real persons or events is purely coincidental. Although reference is made to real celebrities, their dialogue, actions and context in which they are portrayed are all products of the author's imagination.

All That Glitters. Copyright © 2009 by Veronica Patrice. All rights reserved. No part of this book may be used or reproduced in any form or by any means including electronic, mechanical, photocopying or stored in a retrieval system without written permission except in the case of brief quotations embodied in critical articles and reviews. For more information e-mail PaperCut Publishing Inc. at: veronica.patrice@ymail.com.

PaperCut Books may be purchased for educational, business or sales promotional use. For more information please write: Special Markets Department, PaperCut Publishing Inc. at veronica.patrice@ymail.com.

First Edition

Cover Designed by Veronica Patrice
Interior text designed by Veronica Patrice

Library of Congress Cataloging-in-Publication Data

Veronica Patrice
All That Glitters/ by Veronica Patrice._2nd Edition

ISBN: 978-0-615-25242-1

Grand-mommy,

The hardest thing to say is good-bye and since I didn't get a chance to tell you good-bye
I want you to know I will always love you and I will never forget you
You were more than a grandmother you were more like an inspiration to me
You were an incredible woman; one of a kind and no one can ever replace you

I thank god for giving me your strength and because of you I am independent
The shoes you wore were definitely big so I wonder how do I walk behind you
Better yet how can I become half of the woman you were and still be "tippin."
You were an amazing daughter, sister, friend, wife, mother and lastly grandma

Dementia stole your mind and it shattered my heart when you didn't know who I was
In my heart I knew you couldn't have forgotten me completely
And you didn't; the very next day as I walked into your room you shouted Veronica
You then told me you loved me and I will always save that as my last memory

~Rest in Peace~

This book is dedicated to the greatest Mommy and Daddy of all time. Nothing is always sweet but in my life you have always taken the bitter with the sweet and this dedication is just a token of my appreciation.

Love always,

Sweetie Pie A.K.A Boogie

Dear God,

Thank you for holding me down as always because I do not know where I would be without my faith. I do believe but sometimes I get distracted from what could happen. Please watch over my Mommy & Daddy because their happiness means the world to me.

Faith on Hold

His eyes are the windows to his soul
Completely baring the untold
As I watch his heart unfold
My body goes completely cold

What I see frightens me
It not only frightens me but it enrages me
Visions rush my mind that I can't defeat
All because I glanced into his eyes

So now I choose to avoid his eyes
I choose to silence my cries
It's easier to fight these demons if I close my eyes
But the nightmares takeover forcing tears from my eyes

As I take a shot of Patron my eyes become easier to close
I no longer fear the untold
The inevitable may happen but now my heart is froze
And now I'm convinced the pain in his eyes I don't want to know.

Acknowledgements

First and foremost I would like to thank God for he is the reason why I am able to voice my story. He has given me the strength to press on when I honestly felt I had no reason to. Next I would like to thank my Mommy because you are the epitome of what a mom is and I am so proud to be your daughter. I may be a daddy's girl but I'm still my mommy's sweetie. Daddy I appreciate your strength and intentions. You always seem to think of me first even when you are going through so much. I love you!! Every misstep is a lesson learned and you all taught me how to get up, brush off the dirt and keep striving. Thank you and I sincerely hope that I make you all proud!!!

To my Auntie Mary, I love you for being the nicest woman I have ever known, you will never ever be replaced. Don't forget my plate. Ha!! I cannot mention my Auntie Mary without mentioning my Auntie Geraldine. This book may be a little racy for you but thanks for treating me with the same love and nurture as you did your own children. To my cousin Sheree, I thank you for holding me down at CWD; I would not have made it without you. You are truly an inspiration and I wish you much success in every venture you attempt. (See you in Paris) Also don't let Cruella drive you crazy. LOL!!!

To my Grand mommy, I will always love you and you are the reason why I am "tippin'". (Rest in Peace) To Granny, I love you and I will be down there soon. To my little sisters Nichole and Nadine I love you and no more babies please. (WAIT!!) The both of you keep doing big things!! To Keisha, I am still a little mad about the French fries but I guess I still love you. Ha!!! To Lamere, Laquira, Terrance (a.k.a. Lemuel), Titus (my Snickers) and Tyrell I love you all but stop growing; you all are really making me feel old. To Dr. Pamela Nichole Graham we do not talk as much as we used to but my love and support has never changed. I love you and I am only a phone call away.

As a whole I would like to thank the rest of my family because just trying to name half of you is a book within itself. To all of my friends I love and appreciate each of you. Shouts out to Big Boy for being one of the coolest dudes I have ever known. Even though we beef sometimes its all love. Steve, I know you are not going to like everything that I said but I had to keep it real. I know that we are on a different level now so time will tell if its destiny.

I would also like to thank my ex boyfriends and ex associates. I would say names but you all do not deserve that kind of shine besides all of you are old news. Holla!!

To all of the loved ones who have departed us, Rest in Peace: Abraham & Annie Mae Redding, Bobby-Lee Pope, James Redding, Maggie Mitchell, Henry Wooten, Andre Morris (Too Cool for Life) and Courtland Simms; you all will never be forgotten.

If I did not mention your name please blame my mind and not my heart. And last but not least I would like to give a special thank you to everyone who purchased this book. Your support has helped a young girl become a woman.

P.S. To my enemies of the past, present and future, I would like to thank you for your hate. Your distaste for me motivates me to achieve, succeed and excel in whatever I desire. Also you were even better material. Smooches!!!!

The Script

The Script Cont'd

Part III:
Flaws & All

Part IV:
Lessons Learned

Who Am I
101

Some said my skin was too dark to be me. Others said if I lost a little weight I could be a better me. There were even some who thought if I altered my lips or lighten the dark circles around my eyes I could demonstrate true beauty. I often worried about my "big feet" and the braces on my teeth because that was not what I perceived as beautiful. I have finally realized that all of those so called "bad things" are me and are the things that have made me into the woman you now see. Many claim to not be familiar with her so allow me to reintroduce Veronica Patrice exposing the good, bad and ugly.

I consider myself a diamond in the rough because behind the glitz and glam is a heartbroken little girl. I have kept my true emotions buried from even myself. But today I will reveal some of my deepest and darkest secrets. Trust, it is virtually unfeasible to get past my acidic outer without being scorched. In due time, you will witness firsthand a testimony like none other. It is as deep as the bottomless sea and as sweet as pure cotton candy. This is definitely real talk but I had to change the names to protect the guilty and to prevent an ugly lawsuit.

What you are about to embark on are the highs and lows of life, period. Life definitely has a softer side but everyday is not sugary sweet. Some day's feel like you are literally fighting in combat because LIFE is the survival of the fittest. I know everything happens for a reason but I sometimes question the timing. I possess the drive and resiliency of Winnie Mandela yet the creative sense of Gwendolyn Brooks. My words connect with you like Maya Angelou but capture you like Lucille Clifton. The lines clash like Alice Walker yet unite like Graca Machel. The spirit of Nikki Giovanni lingers and is the reason why my revolution is written.

*****Warning*****

This book is a compilation of various experiences I have endured personally and/or witnessed first hand. I love my family and friends but I ask that you not assume to know anything about the particulars of any event mentioned. I guarantee that what you think you know is only absentminded speculation to stir-up confusion and halt my success. Contrary to popular belief I guarantee that will never happen. But I welcome and even encourage you to run and tell that!!!!!!!

Nyame Nti

"By God's Grace"

Part I:
Growing Pains

Walk with me through the heart of the city. Listen to the plea from those who have been deceived, betrayed and forsaken. This is my response to every hater who said I would not or could not because I just did.

~No one can tame destiny~

Veronica Patrice

Veronica Patrice

~~2000, January 3rd

I have come so far but I still have a long journey before me. I sometimes ask myself where I would be without a pen and a pad. Honestly I think I would either be locked up in a mental institution or going to therapy seven days a week. Either way I would not be as happy as I am without my writing. My writing helps me to relax, relate and release enabling me to tolerate all of the struggles in the world. When I am happy; I write, when I am sad; I write and when I am mad; I write. My brain would probably explode if I could not write. I am somewhat of a quiet person and it is sometimes hard for me to express myself to other people. Writing allows me to be myself without the fear of any judgment.

My writing has now giving me the opportunity to relay my experiences with an audience. As an only child I did not have an older brother protecting me, nor a big sister advising me. I did have my mom and dad but you cannot talk to them about everrrything. I had to learn from my own mistakes; a lot of mistakes but they all have made me who I am. If I had a chance to do it all over again I would do everything exactly the same and that is Why I Write.

Why I Write

Why I write this

Is because I lived this

The words that leak from my tongue

Explain exactly where I come from

Why I write this

Is because my lips tighten trying to forget

So without this there is no proof

Only my eyes hold the real truth

Why I write this

Is because you will not simply label me some bitch

My life itself exemplifies so much more

Therefore I have to continue to write more

Why I write this

Is because it is time to do this shit

The gloves are off no more bullshit

I have been waiting too long to for this

Veronica Patrice

Why I write this

Is because I am overcoming this

Pain and struggle no longer run me

I finally recognize my rareness and soon you will love me.

~~2000, March 19th

My life has taken more bumps and turns than any roller coaster. I am constantly on a see- saw; following every highpoint is three low points. Sometimes I wish I could trade places with someone. I know the saying "the grass isn't always greener on the other side" but this just does not seem fair. To outsiders my life appears to be perfect because I grew up in a two-parent household and we were considered "middle-class". I cannot sit here and lie and say my life was horrible but it was a far cry from perfect. It is hard for me to explain my life, but this poem makes it self-explanatory. I think Mary J. said it best:

"Life can be only what you make it

When you're feeling down

You should never fake it

Say what's on your mind

And you'll find in time

That all the negative energy

It would all cease

And you'll be at peace with yourself

You won't really need no one else

Except for the man up above

Because he'll give you love

"My life, My life, My life, My life"

My Life

My heart is about to explode

I feel the pressure penetrating through my skin

I thought this type of shit didn't happen until I was old

But I'm twenty something and my shoulders feel like I am 99

My body keeps telling me to stop

I am constantly worrying about something

I'm at the point that I would do anything to make the pain stop

I find myself turning to liquor, drugs, pills; anything

I wish someone could feel me, understand what I'm going through

I tried to explain my feelings but everyone down plays it like I'm just trippin'

I used to have it all but in the mist of everything I lost my crew

Now I'm all alone with nothing but my eyes watering

I accept the fact that I have done wrong but I didn't know it was to this extent

I mean damn how much can one person take

I try to talk to my man to let off some steam because sometimes I just need to vent

But it just turns into another argument adding some more bullshit to my plate

I have so many dreams and ideas seeping out of my head

But the stress is building and the stones keep coming

All That Glitters

I am beginning to feel like I would be better off dead

Because my feet are tired of running

This has been the longest 365 days of my life

As soon I get past one curve there are five more bumps I need to get over

I wish this were all a dream and I could wake up in a new life

It's funny because my life seemed like so much more before

I know in life you have to make sacrifices but damn can someone else

Can I breathe? I know the saying what doesn't kill you makes you stronger

If that is true than I should be the heavyweight champion of the universe

Eventually I will get knocked out but no one will be in the ring longer

I'm giving my all kicking, punching and screaming anything so I don't have to leave

If only I had a moment to really appreciate my life, I could feel so blessed

Which I am, but I cannot focus on the good because all I can see is the negative

I am so tired of being disappointed, frustrated and depressed

I wish someone would really listen to me, hear me really before there is no me

I have never been so serious about anything in my life

If you care about me reach for my helping hand and lead me

Because I honestly don't know how much more I can take of my so-called life.

~~2001, June 4th

For some strange reason I am always getting called stuck up. But for an even stranger reason I take it as a compliment. I demand and deserve respect so if that makes me stuck up, so be it. Men and women have called me stuck up, but why. Is it because I walk into a spot knowing that I'm fly and couldn't care less about anyone else? Or is it because I keep my hair and nails done, not for show but for me? Maybe it is the fact that when brothers come at me with tired ass game I reject them without the blink of an eye.

I do not need to settle for ANYTHING and that includes my relationships and friendships. If you cannot respect me then FUCK YOU and keep it moving. You do not have to like me but you will respect me. The following is a conversation between an ignorant ass brother and me. He feels that I am stuck up, maybe so but what do you think?

"Hey girl what's up wit you? I know you gonna let a brotha get that number. Damn you got a fat ass; I mean you really got a nice body on you. So do you smoke or are you a drinker"

"Are you serious???
You couldn't possibly be talking to me
You have to be either high or delirious???"

"You ain't gotta get fly; that's what kills me about you stuck up ass bitches. You think everything is all about you; when you really ain't even all that cute"

Stuck Up

First of all, you really don't deserve a response

But this time I'm going to because I am so sick and tired of this

It makes no sense to me that you don't know how to come correctly

If you would have came correctly maybe I could have declined politely

But sense you didn't, I'm not

Second of all my name is Veronica not baby, honey, bitch or slut

I was given that name at birth and that is what I respond to

Third of all, why does my disinterest in you make me stuck up

As if there is something wrong with me when it is actually you

I know you see no wrong in you but who appointed you god's gift to women

Approach is everything and first impressions are unforgettable this applies to both men and women

Because I hate it when women insolently stare at me but cannot give me a proper tribute

Game recognize game; I have no problem giving props where props are due

I'm not asking for everyone to roll out the red carpet but you can at least acknowledge it

Since apparently you liked something about me, what is so hard about just being honest?

Especially men because initially you had to have thought I was pretty

So how in a matter of minutes do I become ugly

Just because I exemplify confidence doesn't mean I'm arrogant

Veronica Patrice

I have been very blessed but in no way do I think I'm better than anyone

I put my pants on one leg at a time just like you

All I demand is RESPECT because if you respect me then I'll respect you

But don't get me wrong; I have no problem with setting you straight

I have a smart-ass mouth and you're not the only one who can be disrespectful

I've thrown blows with the best so if STUCK UP is all you can come up with

So be it because your words will not stop me nor do they change my mind

I know I'm the shit and you know it too but you're just too insecure to admit it

Don't hate me because I love myself; it's enough of me for everyone to love

So in conclusion who cares if I sound stuck up; I don't.

~~2001, July 12th

My man and I have been together for three beautiful years. Honestly, our time together has been so exhilarating. Like the time when we were both awakened by his baby mama busting out my car windows. Or the time when my best friend's head conveniently fell into his lap and coincidently his pants and boxers had just fallen. These are just a few examples of our happiness but the list can go on and on.

We have been brainwashed into believing that all fairytales end with happy endings like Snow White and Cinderella. On the contrary I have learned that every story whether it be fact or fiction has an inside story. Let's take Snow White for example; she had seven men all at her beck and call but she was never content with them. You see my inside story is that I am in denial; I accept my man's excuses and lies because it is easier to live with him than to live without him.

Fairytale

Once upon a time we were living a fairytale

You were my king and I was your queen

But somewhere we made a wrong turn and lost everything

Love, trust and respect had all failed

Once upon a time I trusted you; I would answer your phone with no problem

But now it's an issue because I answered your phone at 3:00 in the morning

See in the beginning you wanted me to answer because those chicks had nothing on me

But now that you've locked me down its suddenly ok for you to talk to them bum bums

Once upon a time I wanted to show you off to the world

But that was before I began noticing some changes

See I was down for you; I never traded up or switched teams

But it meant nothing because you never really appreciated me as your girl

Once upon a time we were in love

The sight of you alone would give me chills

I could careless if you could pay the bills

All That Glitters

I was simply enjoying how you made me feel, for no reason just because

Once upon a time it was me & you

No one could come in between that; not even your baby mama

The family situation wasn't the best but I honestly never hated your mama

I felt that she did not respect me and unfortunately my distaste for her chipped away at you

Once upon a time when you apologized I would believe you

But after the thousandth time for the same shit I've lost faith in that song

I truly wanted to believe that you had changed but how can you when you're never wrong

But time after time I still went back to you

Once upon a time I was more to you than just incredible sex

The last time we spoke we reminisced about what was but sex was all that you talked about

I believed there was a passion underneath it all but I guess I was just a jump off

What happened to "you're the only one", I guess I was always playing second to the next

Once upon a time I really hated you

I in fact wished the worst for you

At one point I wished death on you

But what's really sad is that after everything I'm still fucking with you.

~~2001, September 23rd

"Act Right" is straightforward and to the point. I am speaking on issues men and women can relate to. For me it is a song of empowerment to women all over. I am simply letting men know our past and what to expect in the future. This is not a male bashing poem so to speak. I am merely stating the facts; it just so happens some men need to be bashed from time to time. By no means am I implying that women are perfect because we do have our flaws. I just want women to recognize their worth and demand men to appreciate it.

It is time for the real men to stand up and man up, your excuses will no longer due. I cannot put all of the blame on the men because we as women have accepted the bullshit. We are no longer looking for a good man we settle for an, all right man. Not today because it is time for all men and women to Act Right.

Act Right

Women it is time for us to begin letting these men know

See they can only do what we allow them

And I have come to the conclusion we are allowing them to take us to a new low

Men cannot live without us so why do we insist on giving our power to them

Truthfully men have been playing us for a long time

If you look back in history you'll see every strong man had a strong woman in his shadow

By no means am I trying to bash women; I just feel it's our time to shine

We have been through so much with little acknowledgment of a battle

But not today because I am taking a stand for all women

It is time for you so-called men to **Act Right**

I respect Betty and Coretta because they were strong and dealt with a lot

They were the wives of two influential black men in our history

The key word is ***wives*** because women now and days seem not to require a lot

I'm not suggesting that all women should run off and marry the first man they see

I'm just questioning why we are so comfortable playing the role of babymama

We need to be more concerned with being the "wife" since we are so content on playing the role

All That Glitters

Basically we have set ourselves up but it's not entirely our fault

Some men have chosen not to take care of their responsibility while some women chose to rely on a pole

But not today because I'm taking a stand for all women

It is time for you so-called men to **Act Right**

Tina is definitely considered a bad sista' and no doubt strong

But no woman deserves to be treated in that way

She supported her man, constantly cleaning up his messes and it has been that way for too long

We continue to let these men drive our self-esteems into the ground but it's a new day

We will no longer be Tina and Halle to our men

I'm not saying they weren't good women but what was ok then is no longer good enough

We as women need to respect ourselves enough to know even without a man we can win

Women endure more than men but we still allow them to make our road rough

But not today because I am taking a stand for all women

It is time for you so-called men to **Act Right**

Not only do men have to respect us but we also need to respect ourselves

We are naturally leaders therefore we should lead by example

And stop anticipating for the next woman to fail

With this attitude we will never reach our goal

This may be a mans' world but a woman is capable of running it

Men seem to be so content with seeing us half naked at the strip club and in music videos

That they in fact missed the announcement that we're now on some new shit

The game has changed and we are no longer secretaries to the CEO's we are the CEO's

Today I am standing with all women saying

It is time for you so-called men to **Act Right!!**

~~2001, November 17th

If I had a good man I would… cook, clean and be no holds bar in the bedroom. Sounds familiar? To familiar but why, why do I have to build myself around him? I have to consider how to get him before becoming the woman I am. I know I am losing some of you, but walk with me. Think about all of the changes we go through to get and keep a man. We keep our hair and nails done while making sure all of the other hairs are cut, shaved and waxed. We sacrifice breathing in order to squeeze into that dress. Those five-inch stilettos that are killing our feet we tolerate. Not only that, in the bedroom we have to be creative, flexible and skilled. After all it is our responsibility to suck him, ride him and put him to sleep.

We all like to pamper ourselves as well as please our men but where do we draw the line. I am not saying doing these things are wrong or that we should stop. I am merely saying when we alter one thing we lose something else. We all know what we would do for love but the real question is what won't you do for love.

Things I Won't Do 4 Love

Loving someone is a sensitive emotion

Giving someone all of you is a difficult position

But playing myself is not an option

See I know my worth so settling is out of the question

I'm a strong woman; I know all that I can withstand

I'm a smart woman; I can do without a helping hand

I'm an independent woman; I do for me without asking a man

I'm an ambitious woman; I overcome without affecting my overall plan

What people don't realize is that you cannot stop me mentally

Physically you can hurt me but it doesn't change how I feel about me

I love myself and I will not let anyone change that about me

There is no price on me but I deserve to be treated better than royalty

I don't have patience; I don't like waiting; but I'm considerate

I don't have sympathy; I don't like excuses; but I'm compassionate

I don't have sensitivity; I don't like sappy; but I'm affectionate

I don't have limitations; I don't like restrictions; but I can adapt

All That Glitters

God made me complex from day one

If LOVE cannot accept me than I'll just have to move on

I represent many but this is my mission

I was put here for a reason I'm not just dreaming

I love tough; I hate tough; but I'm reliable

I work hard; I play hard; but I'm dependable

I work out; I eat snacks; but I'm endurable

I speak out; I talk soft; but I'm respectful

At the end of the day I just do me

It's not an act, need or want

It's just Veronica and all that I'll be

Take it or leave it because this is no front

And these are the things I won't do for love.

~~2001, December 28th

Everything is always sweet in the beginning. He sends you flowers once a week while she plans romantic rendezvous. But where do things go wrong? You were just blowing kisses to one another and now you are seconds from throwing blows. Where did the love go; it was all-good just a week ago but what happened. Did something change? Did he become someone else? Or did she? The correct answer is none of the above because zebras cannot erase their stripes and the same goes for both men and women.

Love can be powerful especially in the beginning. The little things he used to do are no longer cute. Remember how his cooking would leave you speechless; compelling you to be his dessert but that never bothered you. Now a year later dinner is still nice but why can't he do the fucking dishes. Remember when she would make love to you everyday but now you are left asking, can I get some this month. Love can take you through so many changes, some are good and others are bad but you can always reminisce about What It Was.

What It Was

See it was real

It was suppose to be for life

I guess it really wasn't a big deal

After all it ended up being a big lie

Remember what you used to say

How about the way you used to act

Or even the promises you gave

Maybe it was my fault for accepting the lies as facts

I don't know, but that was what it was

See we used to be tight

Respect had never been an issue

I guess things were never right

Because look at the shit between me and you

Remember our long talks at the Royal

How about all of the plans we had made

What happened to you being loyal

How could your love just fade

I don't know, but that was what it was

Remember when we were everlasting
Or, at least I thought we was
But truthfully I don't know what happened
We used to be all kisses and hugs
But now I cannot even talk to you
You do'nt even talk to me
I guess it wasn't that important to you
Why not just return keys and let what is be

I don't know, but that was what it was

We were supposed to be over
We were really not supposed to be here
I guess we weren't supposed to be lovers
Maybe love was never supposed to grow here
I really don't have a clue; I can ask myself that question all day
But I still don't have the right answer
I just hope one day I actually find what I thought I had

But truthfully I hope I find a whole lot more

I don't know what it was, but I now know this is what it is.

~~2002, January 2nd

When I was a young girl I idolized Michael Jackson. He was so cute then and he could dance his ass off. My world drastically changed when Ms. Jackson hit the scene. She was young, pretty and could sing and dance. But what I liked about her most was the fact that she was a girl. Janet showed me that girls could do what guys did and sometimes better. To me she was the girl version of Michael Jackson. I can still remember how I felt the first time I heard her album. I knew then she would be my idol and the song "Control" would be my anthem.

"This is a story about control
My control
Control of what I say
Control of what I do
And this time I'm gonna do it my way
I hope you enjoy this as much as I do
Are we ready
I am
Cause it's all about control
And I've got lots of it"

Control

At all times I must contain it

It's something I will not share

I'll do anything to maintain it

Test me if you dare

I refuse to give anyone the opportunity

To take responsibility for my demise

When I fail the blame falls on me and only me

But to your surprise

Bumps in the road will not stop me

They may delay or slow me down

But there's not much that can flat out hold me

There's always a smile behind my frown

I truly understand its importance

I can see why we constantly fight for it

Because living without it is like being caged in a fence

And naturally you would do anything to get out of it

The person who has the most of it

Has the upper hand and a bad hand at that

Not bad meaning bad but bad meaning good can you follow it

Veronica Patrice

Maybe I'm going too fast, let me take a sec and bring it back

When you have it you're left to make all of the decisions

Or you can decide someone else has to

Either way it's all up to you and your expectations

You have the right to accept or decline there's no longer a "have to"

The key to living with it successfully is being able to give in

This is primarily where my problem exist

I cannot seem to let it go, it's like I need it to win

In the back of my mind I think someone will stab me in the back with it

I guess it mainly boils down to an issue of trust

If you trust someone enough than you can trust they won't hurt you

But when you cannot trust that person you don't necessarily know what is just

You cannot see the positive because the negative blinds you

I need someone to show me how to deal with it

School me to opening my heart so that I'm able to let it go

Everyone looks to me for the answer but why when I still question it

What do they expect me to say besides "I don't know"

I acknowledge my mistakes I just need someone to show me how to correct it

Maybe then I won't be so affected by it

Someone needs to take control because I'm not ready to give it

But if someone steps up and takes it then I'll know I don't need all of it.

~~2002, February 20th

Love is funny it can make you do some of the craziest things. At one time or another we all have said or done something that we once said we would "never" do. Until you are personally affected by a specific situation you never know what you might actually do. I have never been a victim of domestic violence but I have witnessed domestic violence first hand.

I never understood how a woman could allow a man to hurt her physically and/or emotionally. Initially I blamed the women because I believed they choose to settle and/or accept what was being given to them. As I have gotten older I realize the power of love and how it can change your perspective. When you are in love the negative things for some reason don't look as bad but the good things look so good that the bad is no longer visible.

Hands on Me

I used to love the way he touched me

The way his hands caressed my body

His hands always seemed to have this crazy affect on me

Whatever he wanted and/or desired I would always comply

You see I once believed that we had something special in which we did

But I wanted it to be more than something physical

Because when he spoke I never listened but whatever his hands directed me to do I did

I know this shit sounds crazy even somewhat whimsical

But what can I say I loved his hands on me

Even when we made love his hands had this way of pulling me

He would hold me down and even push me but I knew he would never hurt me

Occasionally he could get a little too rough but I would always let him get the best of me

But shit was not always peaches and cream we would argue about damn near everything

But I never left him even when I tried he only had to touch me to stop me

He would throw me down and make love to me over and over again

But today is different because I wake up with different hands on me

You see these hands no longer caress me they abuse me

I used to cry tears of ecstasy but I now cry because fist are whaling at me

The words leaving his mouth are still dirty but the delivery is more piercing to me

I'm now left wondering how could he put his hands on me.

~~2002, April 27th

There are many forms of dance such as ballet, salsa, ballroom and the most intriguing of them all, exotic dancing. You may not consider exotic dancing a legitimate form of dance because of its provocative suggestions but what form of dance does not exhibit some form of sexuality. Some people feel exotic dancers are degrading themselves while others say it is simply a sign of empowerment. I stand somewhere in the middle because there are some instances where it can be seen as degrading but on a few occasions I can see where it is empowering.

What is so captivating about exotic dancing? How does a provocatively dressed woman dancing on a pole exemplify power? Well it is simple; she is powerful because she has complete control. She has the ability to make your mate spend their bill money and even their rent money just to continue their fantasy. There are neither boundaries nor restrictions to what she will do. She is turned on by her power so much that it is almost as good as the sex and money.

Dance for Me

Damn, I'm a bad bitch

5'8 with skin like chocolate ever so rich

The curves are like waves in every switch

It's not game I can simply scratch any man's itch

I've discovered a talent for taking anything I want

And I do mean anything, which includes your husband remember it's no holds bar

I have him so infatuated with me that my presence alone will make him cum

I transform each of his fantasies into reality leaving him praying for more

But his prayers are always answered since he has yet to miss a session with me

Everything is standing at attention at the mere sight of me

I am what he desires; I am his fantasy to which he spare's no expense

I supply him with a service in dollars never cents

Whenever he comes home know he has already came, literally

I am his breakfast, lunch and dinner or whatever snack he needs

I can either be carried out or delivered to his door promptly

With me his dream never has to come to an end as long as he pays the fee

I have him truly believing that it's only he

But what he doesn't know is that I have an abundance of fans

All That Glitters

I give him the confidence to perform with me on higher level than you

I have him open for anything because I've conquered what's in his pants

Some say the way to a man's heart is through his stomach but that's not true

There's a McDonald's on every corner the secret is in what you do

Because what you will not do I prefer to do

There are times when he just needs to vent so I let him complain about you

This is where I prosper; I put on my best show forcing him to forget all about you

It's nothing personal but I have a job to perform

And I always perform to the best of my abilities

All of my services are accompanied with a lifetime warranty guaranteeing satisfaction

There's no need for refunds because I always execute accurately

Know that replacing me will indeed be a difficult task

Feel free to try but I'm the only reason why he screams Dance for Me.

~~2002, July 14th

This is an ode to all hustlers' girlfriends because once upon a time I was a d-boy's girlfriend. In the beginning all I could see was the glitz and glam of it. I had to learn the hard way about the sleepless nights and late night booty calls. Being with the man on top indeed had its advantages but they did not compare to the pain I began to feel. I fell in love with him and his lifestyle. I found myself accepting a lot of bullshit just because I enjoyed living the "good life". My bills were always paid and I was able to go shopping whenever I felt. But I now realize I treasured those material things more than I treasured myself.

Everything was fine until he had gotten locked up. Now the tables have turned, what am I supposed to do? Of course he expects me to do his bid with him and hold him down. But what about all of the sleepless nights and booty calls? He tells me everything will be different when he comes home. Like a dummy I believed him and now I am determined to hold it down until he is released. I risked my life and freedom for him but guess what he did once he was released; the same sleepless nights and booty calls. Finally after the third and fourth bid I realized he was never going to change and I walked away from everything; I left him and the money.

Inmate# 47829

Isn't it funny how jail changes your perception

All of a sudden now you realize how much you love me

But I see through it; I know your true intentions

You're just lonely; you don't really care about me

Those four walls are silent, so you sit there reminiscing

Remembering how down I was for you and how you continually played me

Now you finally see what you've been missing

You see the mistakes you've made and how they hurt me

I guess I'm supposed to forgive and forget; act like there was never any drama

You want me to be cool with accepting all of your collect calls

And making three-way calls to all of your different babymamas

Yeah right, did you give a fuck when you fucked around on me

We both started out with no kids, I still have none but you have three

But you expect me to hold you down since now you realize how much you love me

Man you've called the wrong one

I'm not accepting shit; call the fishes you cheated on me with

When everything was sweet they were clinging to your nuts, where are they now

Veronica Patrice

Oh, now they mean nothing and I'm the only one you want to be with

Right, everyone you played me for left you for dead

Yet you still have the audacity to ask me to be there for you

Hell no, because I wasn't enough for you to stop jumping from bed to bed

I must admit you did have it good; I was so in love with you

There was nothing I wouldn't have done for you

But you took advantage of me and only cared about you

So FUCK YOU, I've moved on and now it's time for you

You put everyone above me

And now since you don't have anyone

You want to look to me

But you burned that bridge; I'm not the one

Keep it moving good luck with your journey

I told you time and time again they didn't really care about you

Where were they when you were broke and didn't have any money

They couldn't have cared less about you, but I stayed around

Babymama number 1; I left for a minute, but like a dummy I came back

Babymama number 2 and 3 I found out about at the same time but I still stayed down

Who knows about the countless others, but I always had your back

All That Glitters

But it was never enough; you wanted what I could no longer be

I'm tired of playing second, third and forth to your hoes

All they did was use you, I always held my own, but it took nothing for you to play me

I stayed with you for the highs and lows

But what did I reap, nothing, I have nothing to show for besides pain

You changed me, made me someone else; it took me a long time to love again

I tried to hate you but I still loved you so I accepted the call when I heard your name

But once you began talking I realized I couldn't go through this again

I cannot believe you really thought you could just come back like that

I accepted your bullshit for too long just like I accepted this phone call

But the next time you call I'm pressing two and don't even bother calling back.

~~2003, January 1st

Everyone has his or her breaking point and I have finally reached mine. I am so tired of my man's games and constant lies. I am so tired of the late night phone calls from various females. I am tired of finding numbers in his pockets and lipstick on his collar. I still love him but I am so fed up with his bullshit. Honestly, I do not believe that he would tell the truth to save his own life.

Ladies why do men always have to have their cake and eat it too? No matter how good they have it at home they desire more. Maybe not all men but most men would prefer a ménage over missionary with even the finest woman. I break my back to please him yet it takes nothing for him to disrespect me. But today I cut all of our ties because I have finally had Enough.

Enough

Finally I've had enough

I'm so tired of all of your games

Why couldn't you just be upfront

And tell me you wanted to hit more than one dame

I mean I don't deserve this, I could've been moved on

If only I knew you were trying to play me like average

I would've been left and stayed gone

But you played with me; every time I let you go you always found some type of leverage

I mean I did whatever you wanted besides fuck myself over

I guess that was what you were waiting on but you never had it coming

Yeah I started slipping but once I realized you weren't going to shield me I ran for cover

It's really fucked up when I needed you the most you left me hurting

You've known me for a long time but you couldn't see I was going through something

It's so funny how you remember all of the bad things I did but see no wrong in you

You know you were dead wrong so don't even try to play it like I'm just bitchin'

Because all you had to do was tell me you wanted your cake and eat it too

All I asked from you was to be real and you couldn't even do that

Veronica Patrice

We were friends before anything but you couldn't call or even send a text message to tell me

I didn't make you commit to me and truth be told I wasn't even ready for that

But you did, you made me promises, you sold me dreams; what could you possibly gain from playing me

I know it sounds like I am pissed off at you, but I'm more pissed off at myself

Everyone else saw it and they tried to warn me but I ignored them because I loved you

I had so many other men campaigning but yet and still I put them on the shelf

I mean we had our issues but you were still my man and I was trying to stand by you

That was my biggest mistake because I should've been stop fucking with you

Being real I should've never started because I knew the type of man you was

You were a hoe then and you're a hoe now! Damn, why did I believe you

I never regret anything but loving you is my first and only regret just because

I knew all along, I knew and I did nothing; I ignored my heart

It told me to leave you alone but for some reason I couldn't or just didn't

I mean the dick was all right but I had better

Even after my own conscience warned me I still didn't listen

But now I know and I guarantee I won't make the same mistake with my next hand

You see this entire hand was pointless because you were never really deserving of me

All That Glitters

All of the time and energy I wasted on you I could've used for the right man

But even still I keep asking myself why, why you, why did I let you, you of all people fuck me

Not literally but why, how, when; I guess I was just trippin'

I mean I had to definitely be smoking something because I was really in love with you

But how when there was no trust and there shouldn't have been since I did catch you cheatin'

But I continually gave you chances so I cannot put all of the blame on you

I was very foolish to ever believe in you so some of the blame falls on me

After everything I stand with my head high because in the end I still shine

I honestly do forgive you and I wish you the best but know that you never got the best of me

So this is goodbye for the very last time

I'm not going to get into the facts of how you will never find anyone better than me

Or how once I'm gone you're going to miss me

Because if you don't already know I guarantee that you'll eventually see.

Veronica Patrice

~~2003, May 19th

Corporate America is a world where everyone is out for him or herself and is willing to do anything to get to the top. I worked in this world but my intentions were different because I did not come to "top" corporate America; I came to learn it. I wanted to have some experience in all aspects of business. I quickly learned corporate America was not for me since I have never been nor desired to be a liar, cheater or backstabber.

I am for the most part an honest person. I am a firm believer of hard work but I do not agree with ass kissing. I also do not condone being phony. I am not referring to the fake voice us as sista's put on to sound professional. I am talking about the office gossip sessions where everyone is talking about everyone but leave the huddle smiling in everyone's face. I do my work everyday but I cannot get a raise because I chose not to bring the boss lunch everyday. There are no guarantees of receiving a turn in corporate America therefore; I have chosen to take My Turn.

My Turn

I will not lie, cheat or suck up to anyone

My intelligence alone should sway you

I do not need to pretend nor fantasize about being anyone

I'm completely secure with myself, unlike you

You can only chase my shadow from afar

Why, because I'm on a level that you have yet to see

You may indeed be older but I'm without doubt wiser

At thirty you have achieved so little compared to my accomplishments at a mere twenty

You're so determined to stop me but you don't realize that you're standing at a standstill

From the day I met you I was ahead of you

Logically you cannot stop me because we're not on the same bill

You're not a threat to me because I've already defeated you

I'm not worried about you nor do I fear slowing down

I sincerely don't see that happening but if I was to

I can afford to because I'm already upward bound

Even with less momentum I'll still have passed you

All jokes aside did you really think that you were my competition

Veronica Patrice

You should be condemned for believing such a ridiculous notion

I don't even see you as competition for a high school student

Seriously what do you have that I don't or for that matter want

I'm riding a 07 Chevy while you're riding a Hyundai and paying rent

Step your game up before you have the audacity to try to compete with me

Even after all of your sabotage you are still left staring at my back

I'm the quick-witted roadrunner while you are the lackluster coyote

This may sound harsh but it was long overdue

Everyone can see through you; you are paper-thin

Remember the golden rule "do onto others as you want done onto you"

Because if you treat everyone like you treated me you will never keep a friend

My initial thoughts of you were so drastically different

I cannot believe I actually fell for your charade

But now I see you for what you really are; nothing

I'm going to blow up in your face like an army grenade

I've revealed my hand to you, yet you still cannot see me

Isn't it sad you've been trying to play a game that has yet begun

You need to see me before you can catch me and touch me before you can pass me

You might as well let it burn because it is now MY TURN.

Nsoromma

"Child of the Heavens"

Part II:
Jane Doe

Expect the unexpected because you really do not know me. You could never know how I really feel because I have never told you. Listen closely as Jane Doe gives you a glimpse of reality.

~Don't knock on doors you don't want opened~

Veronica Patrice

~~1998-2005

Some shit should never be discussed and some events should never be relived. I struggled with what to say and what not to say for this book but this book was created from raw emotion. I honestly did not want to offend anyone or cause people to point fingers at certain individuals. As I said in the beginning do not make assumptions because no poem is about one particular event and/or person. With that said the next few poems need no introduction or story line; it just is what it is.

I Said No

I met this guy

He was somewhat older

But back then that was my type

I was fifteen and thought I was so mature

I wasn't able to date yet

But he was cool with just talking on the phone

For that reason I assumed that he really liked me

He never pressure me so we continued to talk off and on

For some reason we always stayed in contact

I was young so I believed this was fate

But life changed when I stepped into that white Cadillac

That night he picked me up for our first date

I couldn't wait to tell my friends

We didn't have a destination so he stopped at this gas station

Before he got out he asked if I wanted anything

How polite I thought as he reappeared with two bags in hand

I thought to myself damn did he just go grocery shopping

He said we were going to chill at his house and have some drinks

Veronica Patrice

At that point I became nervous because I was never into drinking

But I played it cool not wanting to appear young acting

As I walked into his house there like ten guys there

He told me to sit down but I shied away he caught on though

So he walked me to his room and put the movie Christine in the VCR

He passed me a drink but as I sipped the room began to move

The next thing I remember is him climbing on top of me

But I said No

I remember him forcing himself inside of me

But I said No

It felt as if I was watching a movie

Is this what is suppose to happen

Was this what guys and girls really did

I couldn't move or make it stop but I did say No yet the movie kept playing.

Mommy's Angel

This is what I am

Or at least that's what I've tried to be

I always wanted to be the best daughter

Even though many never paid attention to me

I tried to excel to impress you

I even tried to be disobedient for your attention

I hid my true feelings to prevent hurting you

I later learned how to completely turn off my feelings

Honestly they never really mattered

What's the point in making a big deal

I mean to who everyone replaced my feelings with dollars

So why would anyone care about how I feel

I tried to express myself but no one was really listening

I tried to open my heart to people but they ended up being why I shield it

I am battling with so many things within

I feel guilty for not being able to deal with it

I am strong but not as strong as I pretend

I drink myself into a coma not wanting to cry myself to sleep

I call myself a black angel because my heart is dark

Veronica Patrice

It has been broken into a million pieces

But I'm an angel because my heart can be put back together

When I think no one is listening I know that God is

Sometimes I question it but in my heart I know

I've held in so much pain with no where to release it

To have everything yet have no one is definitely a new low.

Suicide

When I woke up this morning everything was all good

Today's decisions have turned out to be very expensive

I keep replaying the day wondering what did I just do

If only I would've done that but I chose to do this

Honestly I fucked up there's no way around that

Just look at everything I put at risk

From today there's no turning back

I contemplated giving up on it all

Scratch that because that's still an option

I'm just so mad that I'm the reason for my fall

It's not that I'm embarrassed or ashamed

I'm just so disappointed in myself

This should've never been my end result

Though making that phone call was far from easy

It hurt but I played the cards that I dealt

I could've stayed but I feel like I'm going crazy

I can't even bring myself to look at my own reflection

I hate myself; in my heart I feel like I don't deserve to be here

I wish I could turn back the hands of time

Veronica Patrice

I promise that my choices would be different

I can't eat, sleep or think about anything else

For the first time in my life I don't yearn to write

Suicide has become my addiction just the thought itself

I feel so caged because my thoughts are now so constricted

And today my heart killed me

It killed my future and my dreams with one decision

That one mistake now consumes me

Death is all that I can envision

I can see no tomorrow; I no longer aspire to be anything

I'm just along for the ride with no way home

What's really the sense in living

When I can't even forgive myself for what I've done

All that I have left is a body with no soul

Once upon a time I had faith

But now my heart is ice cold

And today my heart committed suicide.

D.I.A.M.O.N.D.S

Destiny~**I**nnovates~**A**mbition~**M**otivation~**O**bstructs~**N**egativity~**D**isplaying~**S**incerity

Diamonds are a girl's best friend

Yet so much blood can be found on them

We are killing each other to make this acquaintance

Honestly no one can really afford them

Not long ago I wanted the biggest one

But I now see that we have a lot in common

My life seems so perfect and fun

Sure I have a nice car, good job and even a few diamonds

But there is great pain and agony behind my smile

People are dying for the karats I now desire

But their beauty is actually a façade not a simile

If you look deep into my eyes you'll see the fire

It's the same fire that you hear from the rebels in Africa

You see their blood stains the sand

And my tears drench my pillow

But we fight on with somewhat of a plan

Even though our pain runs deep much of it is self afflicted

They could easily stop killing each other

But diamonds are a girl's best friend

Veronica Patrice

The same thing they're dying for I ironically live for.

Envy Me

I envy me

The me everyone else sees

The incredible me

Who everyone seems to need

They claim I'm so strong

But why do I feel so weak

How can they be so right and I be this wrong

Even after falling to my many defeats

People still claim to envy me

Don't get me wrong I know I'm fabulous

But the level others set is too high

I actually agree that I'm above average

Saying otherwise would be a bold face lie

Honestly all that swag is actually me playing a role

I'm not naturally that confident

My personality is not always so bold

Veronica Patrice

Sometimes I can't do nothing but envy me

I walk with my head high

But I don't always know the way

I cover my insecurities with what I buy

Never show face regardless to what others say

I've never been the type to put others down

Hating on the next really doesn't do anything for me

Yet people still claim to envy me

I do aspire to be that me

Honestly I want to better me

I want to trump what everyone expects of me

The sky won't even be big enough to hold me

Oprah status wouldn't seem so foreign to me

But I'm on my way so look for me

And people will have a reason to Envy Me.

Double-Dutch

I love him but he's not the one

Although he serves his purpose

Two is always better than one

Playing the fence made me nervous

But then I became excited

The trill of having my cake and eating it too

With a glass of milk on the side

Was too much pass and not enough to outdo

Each had their flaws but the good outweighed the bad

My main line is the perfect husband and family man

He has a house, car, job and no baby mama attached

But my side piece lives in the hood and has no plan

He has three little ones that claim his last name

I know what you're thinking easy decision

Not exactly because the "d" puts him back in the game

Sex isn't everything and my main line can hold his own

But I just can't walk away from my side piece

The only thing I fear is getting caught up

I love my main line but I'm in love with the "d"

Veronica Patrice

Fuck playing with fire I'm playing double-dutch

I'm jumping in between two ropes trying to keep up

Remembering birthday's and anniversaries

Baby names and phone numbers

I've had some close calls but I always land on my feet

Still jumping on pace but I'm getting a little tired

My moves aren't as smooth as they once were

Those close calls are now becoming more frequent

The ropes have started to twirl faster

The game is changing I think my main line may be creepin'

I found a couple of numbers but no concrete evidence

Now I'm jumping in reverse with the fear of reaping

The inevitable I can't lose my main line over my greediness

Jumping on one foot in reverse I finally trip up

I guess that's what I get for playing double-dutch.

Barry Bonds

I can't stop

But I wanna stop

I wanna quit

But the words don't fit

I'm tired because I've been through so much

I know I have no real reason to fuss

Because I belong here

Even though I sometimes doubt myself I have a place here

I have a purpose here

Yet I'm still ready to leave here

I've worked so hard

But I still don't believe that I belong

I want, dream, believe and deserve this

But a bottle of pills could still end this

The decision I make will make this

Yet I lie here still questioning what is

I'm trying yall I really am

Seriously everyone cheering in the stands I hear you

I may not react quickly enough for you

But I ask that you keep rooting for me

You believed this far so bare with me

Listen closely because my heart is speaking to you

Not out loud but through my actions

Through my heart I plea to you

I beg of you

Lend me your ear for understanding

Not to figure me out but to realize the thing

The thing that makes me

Ironically is exactly what breaks me

My dad is all of me

He is why I still do me

Yet he is the reason why I would give up on me

I sincerely wish that I could take his pain

His hurting body

I wish I could restore

So much of him is me

Therefore, I need strength to be me

I'm not sure if I'm strong enough

But time waits for no one and I'm next to bat

I have no other choice but to hit a home run

And I did just like Barry Bonds.

Daddy's Girl

I am strong because he is

He battles with so much

But still somehow he always thinks of me first

Even before I leave we always depart with a hug

And he still tells me he loves me every time we speak

I love him with all of my heart

But the thought of losing him makes me weak

This poem was the hardest for me to even start

To this day I can still remember the day I made him cry

I hurt him so much that day but I didn't understand back then

How could I be so selfish and only think of I

I'm just sitting here reminiscing on the good times

We had so many do you remember riding the roller coaster with me

Or the time we went swimming at Disney World

And no matter the day or time I could always call you to come and get me

From day one I have always been Daddy's girl

We would watch the game and you'd take me for rides through the city

You would get me ice cream from Joe's like three times a day

But now you have to go dialysis three times a week

And I'm scared I'm so scared that one day

I just can't fathom it

I know I won't be able to handle it

I love you daddy

Always and Forever Boogie.

Sesa Woruban

"I Change and Transform My Life"

Part III:
Flaws & All

Let me start off by saying I am a Leo and my personality definitely reflects that of a Leo. I do have a slight attitude but he finds a way to still love me. I can be harsh and unapologetic but I really do have a heart. Even after everything I have already said you all accept me flaws and all.

~Just do you~

Veronica Patrice

2006, May 16th

Have you ever awakened one morning feeling better than you have ever felt? You could be in the mist of drama but something about this morning is just different. It reminds me of what it feels like when the rain stops in a thunderstorm. The sky is still dark and there may be thundering and lighting but for some strange reason the clouds are dry. This morning I woke up feeling like the world was finally mine to conquer. I felt free of my past and was ready to move on.

The Morning After

I woke up this morning feeling like a brand new person

Everything that has happened prior to today no longer disturb me

Yeah, yeah I know I've said this before but today just feels different for some reason

I think in the past I was forcing it because deep down I really wasn't ready

It's all so clear to me now but prior to today I had given up on everything

I didn't believe in myself or anyone else for that matter

I treated myself like shit because I couldn't get pass the negative things

In life everyone has hardships but I began sinking into mine with no strength to reach for the ladder

I tried to stay focused but everything I was doing was for the wrong reasons

I had something to prove but not to myself it was just for show

I now know what others envision as happiness doesn't have to be my reason for breathing

From now on I'm going after everything I want, wherever my heart sends me is where I'll go

I know this sounds crazy but today I just feel like getting up and walking

See the difference between yesterday and today is that yesterday I was running

I wasn't running from anything in particular I was just running from everything

Everything that could result in disappointment can you believe I used to be driven

Veronica Patrice

I never knew what failure meant because I always had complete control of my situation

It was impossible for me to see failure when success was all I had ever envisioned

And then unexpectedly I lost control with no time to react I barley saw what happened

It was as if I was sitting on top of a hill and all of a sudden I began to roll

Once I began rolling I couldn't stop I just kept rolling through everyone until there was no one left

I knocked them all out of the way and that was when I turned cold

The further I rolled the less I sought to stop because I realized there was nothing left

After rolling and rolling I finally hit a big ass tree, thank God for that tree

Because it made me stop and look in the mirror and face the demons I once tried to forget

It sounds a lot easier on paper but I experienced feelings you would never believe

Shit I couldn't believe my own transformation because I was always the one less affected

I thought I didn't let things get under my skin but I guess I thought wrong

Because I was feeling all sorts of pain, resentment, anger, frustration and just flat out loneliness

I continuously reached out to people but they just kept disappearing leaving me all alone

I couldn't understand why they left but the real question is why did I need them

This morning I feel strong enough to face things on my own

I didn't hit rock bottom but I damn sure came close luckily my cries didn't fall on deaf ears

I was finally free, free to rise, free to pick myself up and start back up the hill

But before I climbed up the hill I closed my eyes and went to sleep

And before I had awakened God's hands picked me up and I began to climb The Morning After.

~~2006, May 29th

Have you ever had a schoolgirl crush but you are no longer a schoolgirl? The new man in your life makes you feel like you are still in high school. You all talk for hours and even argue over who should hang up first. This man has you truly believing you are a born again virgin. You have only known him for a couple days but you swear it is love.

How could you love a man you have only known for some odd days? It sounds impossible to think I am in love with a stranger. But he is not a stranger I feel like I have known him my entire life. It is as if we have already met in another life because he knows everything about me. I did not believe in love at first sight until now because I am convinced I have just found my soul mate.

Schoolgirl Jones

Damn I feel like a schoolgirl

This brotha really has me jonesin

I think I'm falling in love; I'm not sure but I don't feel like the same girl

I still cannot believe he has me this open and this soon

I'm feeling him so much that I didn't even bother to ask if he had a woman

I had always dreamed my prince would come and sweep my off of my feet

But I never thought like this, he picked me up and has yet put me down

I'm floating on cloud nine; whenever I'm with him my heart skips a beat

The sound of his voice alone makes me blush

Sometimes I wonder if he's too good to be true

I never imagined I could feel like this from one man's touch

We have yet to be intimate but he has me seriously questioning what my body might do

I find myself daydreaming of what could be

Picking out baby names and wedding dates

How can I feel like this after everything my ex did to me

I don't know but hopefully this is my fate

Veronica Patrice

Even still it's way too early for me to be feeling this way

But for some reason I can't control it; somehow I fell victim to cupid

And I've been head over hills ever since that day

Ever since the arrow pierced my heart I've been clueless about what to do

I don't want to scare him but I need to know if this is real

But then again I don't want to know because it feels so good

I can't stop myself from sometimes questioning if in fact this is the real deal

But I'm going to follow my heart because everything that happens is supposed to.

~~2006, September 21st

What is the difference between love and lust? That is the million-dollar question and luckily I have the million-dollar answer. Many people have mistaken the two for one another but there is a vast difference between the two. Lust is a very strong attraction between two people mostly physical. But "true" love is wayyyy more complicated and cannot be turned on and off as easily. You have no control over love; you cannot chose who, when, where or why. True love is an intoxicating emotion that cannot be understood unless you yourself have experienced it. True love is what keeps you around when he is fucking up. True love is being able to accept the good with the bad.

True love can have many positive views but with anything there are negative instances. For instance, true love made me follow my man and check his phone. Just like true love made me beat that bitch's ass. Nothing in love is perfect but when you are really in love you go that extra mile. My man and I have definitely had our ups and downs but I would not trade him for the world and that is True Love.

True Love

Love is something we have no control over

We cannot dictate who, when, where or why love hits

But when you fall in love you have no desire for another

Outsiders may tempt you but real love is rich and they're merely counterfeits

I never thought I would fall in love again after my ex

I knew someone was out there, I just didn't believe it would happen this soon

Love found me and has yet let me go I'm just holding on anticipating what's next

He came out of nowhere and began patching up my wound

I'm so crazy in love; I cannot picture myself without him

I thought I knew love but nothing has ever come close to feeling like this

I don't know what has come over me but it only happens when I'm near him

Sometimes it makes me mad that he has me so sprung like this

But I get over it quick because I don't want him to ever leave

I even find myself sometimes trippin' on him but lord knows I don't want to lose him

I love everything about him, mentally and physically

I guess he was feeling me too because he asked me to marry him

Of course I said yes but I wondered were we moving too fast

All That Glitters

My mind was telling me to slow down but my heart was telling me to jump the broom

I want to do everything right this time because I really want this to last

Don't get me wrong we have arguments but it never gets too out of hand

I can talk to him about any and everything

He is my best friend and my to be husband

I trust him but sometimes my mind starts wandering

But he always reassures me I have nothing to worry about

He gives me a certain confidence about myself no other man has

I'm no longer worried about if we're moving too fast

Because I now know our love is true love and it will always last.

Veronica Patrice

~~2007, April 14th

Being a young black woman to many may seem like a burden but to me it is where my strength and ambition stem from. It is so easy to fall victim to your circumstances which it is why it takes an extremely strong person to persevere. There were times when I did not feel like I was neither the prettiest nor the smartest but I found a way to press on and find success.

Confidence is very important in any girls' life but especially a black woman's because the odds of being successful are very slim. Black men have been known to degrade us and treat us as if we were not good enough. They all scream they want that "ride or die" chick but once they "blow up" they slither to the other side. I am not trying to make this a black and white issue but regardless to what is thrown at us a stand-up woman stands.

Stand-Up Woman

When the chips fall

And the shit hits the fan

When there's no one to call

And no one to lend a helping hand

I Stand

When the odds are stacked against me

And my back is pinned against the wall

When friends and family abandon me

And others stay scheming; anticipating my fall

I Still Stand

When giving up seems like my only option

And surviving seems worst than dying

When dreams become farfetched notions

And spirits are all you have to stop the crying

Somehow I Still Stand

When waking up becomes a nightmare

And going to sleep becomes an illusion

When everything seems to be unfair

When you can't win for losing

I Still Stand

When no one seems to be listening

And everyone else has fallen

When the diamonds are no longer glistening

And there's no longer a reason to keep pushing

I Stand

When everyone has betted against you

And you almost count yourself out

When opportunity seems to always pass you

And these words are your only way out

I Stand

No matter what obstacle I'm up against

No matter who said it couldn't be done

I guarantee I'll find a way to overcome this

And for that I am a Stand Up Woman.

~~2007, May 6th

The life expectancy of a black man is barely seventy years old. Ten million blacks in the United States currently live in poverty. What do these numbers illustrate? They illustrate a trend that the black man is a dying breed. These numbers are staggering but it is way more than just "someone doing a bid". These bids are affecting our political stance in America. Thirteen percent of all people who have been disenfranchised (loss of voting rights) are black. In six states the number of black men disenfranchised is 25 percent or more, but in Alabama and Florida it is an astounding 30 percent.

These numbers are not mere coincidences they are proof of a conspiracy. The public school systems in most urban cities are embarrassing. Why? For one it is the lack of money being funded. We have billions of dollars to build more prisons but cannot seem to find any money to build schools. Education is power and if we only represent 18 percent of college graduates with a bachelor degree or higher how much power can we really have? Without a college degree what are the chances of obtaining a job with a salary over $30,000. Not likely so what do you do? How do you take care of your family? We need to continue playing the hand dealt to us but we first need to stop blaming the dealer. We already know the playing ground is not fair but we have to play their game on their terms until we can change the game and force our terms. Playing their game on our terms is a lose-lose; always leaving us Turned Out.

Turned Out

My name is Jason but everyone knows me as Jay

I represent the Cabrini Green projects

I was raised in Chicago but I now reside in New Jersey where I'm awaiting to hear my fate

I've held in a lot but it's time to get some shit off of my chest

So bare with me because I'm a little stressed

I just turned nineteen years old yesterday

But I have no mama or daddy to accredit

I'm not pressed because I've been on my own long before today

So don't give me pity or feel sorry for me

They're not dead literally they're just dead to me

My mom is addicted to drugs and my dad has never seen me

I used to blame him for not finding me

But when I found him he claimed to have never known about me

To this day he still doesn't claim me so basically he disowned me

Whatever because him being here doesn't make or break me

My fate has already been written for me

I probably sound like 60 percent of all inner city youth

Which is sad but what can you expect when even the state don't give a fuck

Ironically this all began with the dad I never knew

All That Glitters

After he left my mom she turned to drugs and barely stayed cleaned long enough to give birth to us

It was my younger brother, Shawn and I, he was 9 and I was 14

All of a sudden one day my mom never came home; she never even said she was leaving

We didn't know if she was dead or alive, we didn't see her until her sentencing hearing

She was sentenced to three years even though it was her first offense

We had nowhere to go since I was already dead to my dad and Shawn's dad was no different

So it was left up to me to take care of my brother and me

I started working at Burger World under the table to pay the rent

I tried to take care of him but child services eventually found out my mom was locked up

We were going to be separated unless we moved into my aunt Rita's

Quiet as kept she was a recovering crack addict but child services didn't give a fuck

They were just happy they found someone who wanted to take care of us

But she was only interested in the check they promised her every month

Ironically, this is probably what made her relapse forcing us to fend for ourselves again

Burger World couldn't pay all of the bills so I began hustling

It started out as a means of getting extra money but it eventually turned into an addiction

I was failing all of my classes so I dropped out and Burger World was not paying enough so I quit

All I had left was my little brother and the block

Veronica Patrice

I just turned seventeen and Shawn will be turning twelve; time was passing by so quickly

It has almost been three years since we last seen our mother

She was released early for good behavior; she seemed to be on the right track

She found a job, moved into a new housing development and asked us to move in with her

I was kind of skeptical at first but Shawn was so ecstatic that we moved back

With her back in the picture taking care of him gave me the opportunity to begin hustling full-time

I was on the block from sunrise to sundown

I was trying to stack my money because I didn't know how long my mom would stay clean

Even though she had been clean for almost six months

She recently met this dude named Tony at one of her addiction meetings

I couldn't put my finger on it but it was something grimy about him

I told my mom I didn't like him, but she did and they began dating

After a couple of weeks of dating he moved in

She began missing a meeting here and there but insisted she was still clean

All the while Tony had stopped going to his meetings all together and started back using

I knew it was time for us to move but I was too addicted to hustling

I really wanted to believe my mom when she said she was not using

But in my heart I knew and I eventually saw it with my own eyes

All That Glitters

I came home one day to find Shawn injecting her arm with heroin

I could've killed her but I didn't want Shawn to see her die

He thought he was giving her some medicine; he had no clue she had just used him

He wanted to stay but I made him leave with me

We didn't have enough time to get our stuff but I had planned to go back once we got a room

Shawn finally fell asleep and I went back to my mom's house to get our things

When I walked into the house I found my mother passed out and my room door open

I walked into my room and found my things thrown all around

My money was stashed in a broken floor board so when I seen it standing up I panicked

I ran over to find it empty; not even one dollar could be found

The next thing I knew I was shaking my mother in the air like a maniac

It took everything in me not to kill her I repeatedly asked her where was my money

All she could say was Tony's name and how sorry she was

She was so pitiful I just dropped her on the floor and left to go find Tony

I searched every alley, homeless shelter and crack house but no one knew where he was

He had stolen almost sixteen grand from me, what was I supposed to do now

All I had left to my name was four grand and a couple grams of dope

That might sound like a lot but when you have a little brother to raise and nowhere to go

You can spend that in a few days especially since I still needed to re-up

Veronica Patrice

If only I could find Tony, he couldn’t have smoked all of the money up

But he did; because I found him in an alley dead, overdosed on heroin

I barley had enough to pay for the room we stayed in every night; everything was fucked up

I couldn't spend enough time with Shawn and the streets kept calling him

He eventually started hustling trying to make some extra money

But he wasn’t built for the game and I knew this; I tried so hard to stop him

But I wasn’t quick enough because a drug dealer eventually killed him over some disputed money

I sit here all alone because everybody is dead and gone

Shawn was my only motivation to go on; I don’t want to go if he can’t go

Looking back on my life I can honestly say that I indeed did wrong

I gave it my all, maybe I did make some bad decisions but no one gave me an instruction book

This was the life chosen for me; I was put in this position with what looks like no way out

I’m not sure why jail had to be my destiny but I now realize the state is who turned me out.

~~2007, July 26th

I never in a million years imagined I could ever be this sprung over a man. However, I did plan to get married and have kids but I never thought love would hit me like this. I honestly cannot believe the words coming out of my mouth but I have learned relationships are hard especially long distance ones.

What would you do if the one you loved were called to duty? Not to another city or state but to an entirely different country. Do you stand by him? These were some of the questions I was faced with when my man told me he had to go to Iraq.

Imagine worrying day in and day out about your man's well being. The worst part is; not knowing, not being able to call him or go check on him. I even wondered if he would be faithful because I would be so far away and there would be other women that much closer. Ultimately, I decided to take a chance on love and I told my man in spite of everything I am still With You.

With You

Whenever things get rough and you don't know the outcome

Look to me because I'll always be there for you

When the odds are stacked against you remember your battle is already won

I know everything will work out because the story was written for me and you

When you left Detroit to go to Florida I was hurt but I believed in you

And on this next journey you still have nothing to worry about because I still have your back

Nothing between us will change; you won't stop loving me and I won't stop loving you

Our love has no boundaries and I'll never forget you whether you go to Korea or Iraq

I know you have to go but don't forget you have someone to come home to

I'm going to pray for you but you have to be strong for me

You cannot keep me worrying about you like this

I know you may be scared but you have the strength to conquer all and come back to me

Even if you come back crazy I'm still going to greet you with a kiss

I've told you a million times I'm not going anywhere

Seriously, think about everything we have been through this year

We have been together for one year and counting; it hasn't been perfect but we're still here

We're still in love and still fighting because all of this bullshit just makes us stronger

It hurts sometimes but it feels good to move on to the next chapter

So there's no need to worry lets just focus on making this chapter better

We take a lot of things for granted and no one knows exactly how long we'll be here

But I do know until I breathe my last breath I'll be with you

I will always love you and I will always stand beside you

We may argue and cuss each other out but I will always ride for you

Don't worry about leaving; focus on coming home to everyone waiting for you.

~~2007, September 29th

True friends are hard to come by. I know this because I only have a few of them. Recently I had a disagreement with one of my closest friends. It has almost been two years and we have yet spoken to one another. The reason we stopped speaking was over a man, he was neither my man nor hers but lines were still crossed. I can admit that I am not perfect; I do hold grudges and I do not forgive easily but the blame is not all on me.

Getting into my inner circle is a very difficult task but being cut from it can be done quite effortlessly. Like most people I do not like pain and if I feel you are trying to hurt me or play me I will cut you from my team. However, if you are on my team I will ride for you be it right or wrong but I aspect the same in return. Like I said me and my girl have not spoken in almost a year and we have known each other for most of our lives. Honestly I do not know if we can ever be as close as we once were. But even still I have so much to say that was never said. Therefore, I dedicate this next poem, To Whom It May Concern.

To Whom It May Concern

I remember when we were down for one another

Maybe down isn't the right word but no matter the situation I would always ride for you

We were cousins but you were more like my sister

We've had our ups and downs but somehow we always remained cool

But not this time; I guess this was the straw that broke the camels back

Because we haven't spoken in months but ironically you discuss me regularly

I guess everyone is lying because you would *never* talk about me behind my back

Even amongst the bullshit I've never thrown dirt on your name it was never necessary

Seriously why would I talk shit about the same bitch I would've died for yesterday

Which brings me to wonder why it's so easy for you to talk shit about me

If you had a comment on something or a question regarding someone you could've asked

We've been cool for over twenty years did you really think it wouldn't get back to me

I expected more from you, I expected you to keep it real with me way before any man would

Especially since the man in question wasn't my man but you still knew we had history

I've never kicked it with any of your ex's but if I did you would've been the first to know

The crazy part is that you told me you seen him so why would you leave out the real story

Veronica Patrice

Was giving him a couple lap dances and leaving the club together not important

You claim he was only giving you a ride but where does the bottle and after-hour spot fit in

Oh but wait according to you those things still have no significance

Not even if the man in question was trying to get back with your best friend

Don't get it twisted I wasn't mad about the two of you being intimate

I was more so pissed because after everything you were still campaigning for him

You were suppose to have my back but this wasn't the first time your motives were questioned

And for that reason we have not spoken but everything happens for a reason

Hopefully one day we can get back tight be it five or twenty years from now

I must admit my intentions were drastically different when I first began this poem

But I now realize that life is too short and no one is promised tomorrow

So regardless of what went down I still love you and I'll always be down.

~~2007, October 13th

Have you ever had a dream so good that you swore it was real? Or you just really wanted it to be real because it was that good? You even try to hurry up and go back to sleep to somehow get back to that dream but it is nowhere to be found. The other night I had an experience so good that I could have sworn was real. Now it is definitely possible that I was just missing my man but either way it was the most orgasmic, mind-blowing lustful experience I have ever embarked on. To this day I still do not know what actually occurred but whatever transpired was definitely unforgettable.

A Dime's Dream

I awake from a deep sleep

Drowning in sweat

Shaken and out of breath

With a dude I don't believe to have ever met

Suddenly I fall back and awake

Memories bombard my mind

As to why this man is serving me on a plate

He is tall, black and handsome not to mention all mines

He slowly licks my toes

While gently massaging them he pulls them in and out

His mouth is so warm and his tongue is so soft

He works his way up until my legs spread apart

I lie there dripping wet waiting for the next episode

I watch him move up my thigh with his tongue

I yearn for more and moan ready to explode

But then I feel his fingers slowly approaching

While working his way up 1 piggy 2 piggy 3 piggies he enters

My moans become louder and my hips begin to sway

Then his tongue replaces his fingers

All That Glitters

I'm about to reach my peak I'm only one lick away

Stroke after stroke lick after lick and then I finally explode

But he doesn't stop he just keeps going and going regardless to what I say

Lick after lick, stoke after stroke he continues until his name I scream out

His tongue slowly moves up to my belly button where he teases my upper half

My nipples are hard and full of tension bubbling with anticipation

He continues up my stomach and I begin to laugh

Reaching the fork in the road he goes right taking it all in stride without any hesitation

I began to arch my back in ecstasy while he ventures left

And then I felt his friend slowly graze my middle

It was so hard and ready; he wanted me but he continued to tease me as I pleaded and begged

But there was no need for guiding because it was far from little

And finally we connected I felt him slowly drive himself in

All the while I screamed for him to go deeper

Deeper and deeper I yelled not ever wanting this to end

He pumps harder and faster until his screams become louder

Anticipation builds I feel it I'm almost there

Stroke after stroke I feel him grinding for more

My heart beating fast my body shaking I'm almost there

Veronica Patrice

I reach for him but I don't feel him anymore

I sit up to see what happened, where he went

Then I awake to see there is no one but me

Damn that was a good ass dream.

~~2007, December 18th

My man pisses me off but for some reason I still love him. There are times when I wonder why I am even with him. We go through so much bullshit I wonder is it even worth it. It has gotten to the point that we no longer argue about anything of significance. We now just argue about the outcome of the last argument but for some odd reason I still love him. Listening to this you would never believe we have been together for only two years. We beef like an old married couple but at the end of the day he is my man and I love him.

Sometimes we get so caught up in beefing that we forget why we initially fell in love. He works my nerves and can be very selfish at times but when it comes down to it I know he loves me. My man does a number of things I don't like but there are a million other things that I love which is the reason why I stay.

Reasons

I love him because??

He loves me because???

No matter what he was

Or what I was we're in love so who cares about what was

See I love him from head to toe

He's kind of skinny but he gives me hearty helpings of love

I can ask him for anything without him ever telling me no

He's sexy, strong and smart but he doesn't act like he's up and above

Honestly he doesn't have to act because he has his own swagger

Everything that rolls off of his tongue is seducing

Always leaving me begging for more

The tricks up his sleeve are far from losing

He is every reason why I love him

It's virtually unfeasible for me to name all of them

I know the feeling is mutual because I really believe in him

I adore his mind, thoughts and spirit; I honestly just love everything about him

He is so special; he is my missing puzzle piece

He satisfies me in everyway imaginable

My heart is always open for him therefore he needs no key

All That Glitters

His love for me is always on time and very dependable

When I need a shoulder to cry on I know he is there

When I need someone to talk to I know he will always listen

When I need someone to cheer me up I never call because he already knows to be there

When I need some affection I can always count on his tender kissing

I know it may sound too good to be true

But truthfully that is an understatement because our relationship is that much more

I have yet to touch on what we physically do

But I know life without him would be intolerable

I'm certain that he loves me and I love him to

I could go on and on about our love but these are just a few Reasons.

~~2008, January 27th

I feel like I am running up a steep hill and the top of it is nowhere in sight. I am climbing and climbing all the while jumping hurdles and dodging haters just to be in this same place called nowhere. I am so tired of trying to get to this mystery place called success. I call it a mystery because on television celebrities seem to have everything but they still are not happy. Come to think of it I only have a little "somethin somethin" and even I am not satisfied.

This is primarily why I need to change my way of thinking. From this day forward I am going to focus on how much I have accomplished instead of worrying about how much further I need to go. I know I could have done this and maybe I should have done that but no more I'm just doing me.

No More

There will be no dwelling on what has happened

No more wondering what could've happened

I'm just going to focus on what will happen

And what I need to do to make it happen

There will be no speculation of what should've happened

No more questioning what might've happened

I'm just going to focus on what's going to happen

And what I need to do to make it happen

There will be no regrets of what I did

No more thinking about what if

I'm just going to focus on the good I've did

And how the bad will help me to rise above it

There will be no more uncertainties about if I can

No more doubts about when I can

I'm just going to focus on what I can

And show the world that I indeed can.

~~2008, January 5th

It is funny how poems can come about. "Watch 4 Me" originated from a television special on Alicia Keys. I think it was a show called Ultimate Album on Vh1 for her album, Songs In A Minor. Anyways at the end of the show she said, "In five years watch me, in ten years watch me" and so on. I felt her because I have accomplished so much but this is only the tip of the iceberg. If you are smitten by the fact that I have made it this far then you have no idea what you are in stored for.

I have not done anything as big as A. Keys but I have accomplished a lot of my personal goals. And being real I have almost made it to the sweet part of life. It may not sound like much but the distance in-between bitter and sweet is definitely a journey.

Watch 4 Me

Many have doubted my abilities

They assume I'm glass and one stone can break me

But I'm actually Teflon therefore I'm rarely affected by their negativity
For some reason they love to throw salt on me

But attempting to sabotage my years will not hurt me

Just take a look at my history and you'll see there's no stopping me

All jokes aside the best thing for you to do is Watch 4 Me

You have no control what-so-ever over this

Your whispers of doubt haven't affected a thing

And those threats you keep humming still aren't pressing me

You're basically wasting your time still gossiping

It's really sad it had to come down to this

But I had to pull your card since you mistakenly assumed that I was just talking

He who assumes makes an ass of himself just a quote for future reference

But unfortunately, all you can do now is Watch 4 Me

Know that my time is coming

Respect the intelligence of my mind

Veronica Patrice

Prepare for this strong, black and confident woman

Don't forget I'm always official with mine

You've been forewarned

Even though my presence alone should have been warning enough

I guess you assumed like you, I was playing but this is no game that I'm running

Never under estimate me, take heed to my words and keep watching.

In five years watch me!!

In ten years watch me!!!

In twenty years watch me!!!!

~~2008, February 9th

It is my responsibility as a black woman to acknowledge my history. I know where I come from and I understand my ancestors went through hell for my equality. But it is also my responsibility to let those who do not know, know. It is funny to me that I sit and complain about my life but where would I be if they did not start the battle. How long would I have lasted on the Underground Railroad? Imagine getting beat for no particular reason or roasting in the sun picking cotton all day. How it must have felt to live in a world where you were not even considered a whole person.

If you think your life right now is rough, I guarantee it would not compare to life in the south during the fifties. I am thankful for all of the Civil Rights Leaders and their bravery. They fought for us to have rights, education and careers of the same statue as white people. A lot of rights they fought for we take advantage of, such as voting. I vote faithfully every election and I am a devote democrat. I lead by example and I am guaranteed that my vote will always count.

But what would our ancestors say if they were still living? Would they be ashamed of how black people now portray themselves? I am no one to judge but we shamelessly refer to one another as "nigga", when it was originally used to degrade us. Black women are always screaming for respect but in the same light we are dancing half naked in music videos. Why would anyone respect that? I am not passing judgment on anyone because I've used the word "nigga" before. I also like to dress sexy and Morris Chestnut can get it. But just because I do it does not make it right.

Was It You

Was it you who made me who I am

Or was it the love you've always given me

Was it you who I constantly called to get me out of a jam

And when I did wrong was it you who has always forgiven me

Was it you who stood up for me

All the while they beat you and called you out of your name

Yet you still came for me

And have been my umbrella in the rain

Was it you who loved me

Shown me feelings I never knew

You said you would die for me

And I believed you because of all the things I've seen you do

It was you who made me

Because without you I'm nothing

Your love has carried me

And has been my guide through the hard things

It was you who stood up for me

You marched, fought and made sacrifices in my name

You've paved the way for me

With that I give you praise and fame

It was you who protected me

You've endured so much pain

And now they just look at me

Because we're almost the same

It was you who loved me

You told them they were wrong

You didn't let them hurt me

And for that I am strong

It was you that made me

And your voice spoke up for me

Your hands protected me

And your heart loved me. **-My People-**

~~2008, March 13th

I cannot believe after everything I have been through I am still standing here. Even after all of the mistakes I have made I am still pushing. I began this story as a bitter little girl with a vengeance but I end it as a humble young woman with a purpose. Throughout this story I have openly discussed my insecurities and shortcomings but I intend on ending this chapter on a good note.

I say chapter because I have so many other opportunities awaiting me in the future. I have broken ties with that bitter little girl and I have embraced the woman in me. I have also broken ties with pain, hate and excuses because I no longer need them. In the past I used them as a shield to my heart but that was before I exposed my heart to everyone.

I have no regrets about ANYTHING because EVERYTHING, good or bad has made the woman you now see. I am no longer a diamond in the rough because I have shed the dirt and baggage. My true essence is really that of a rare, flawless diamond. The face people never knew or the name they never remembered is now All That Glitters.

K.I.M

Who knew she held so much power

A woman of her caliber

She intimidates many some even fear her

But that's only because they don't know her

Her name alone invokes discomfort

People don't know how to react to her

Forcing their insecurities forward

Exposing their true emotions for her

Family, friends and associates have all ran into K.I.M

But some people just never learn

The hate is there even before she reaches them

I guess people didn't take heave from My Turn

Even so some will still try to provoke her

They whisper and spread gossip

Not realizing that it doesn't bother her

Nor understanding that playing with her is a costly concept

Veronica Patrice

In hindsight she maintains her cool throughout adversity

Mostly doing so without showing any emotion

She presents the bystanders with a glimpse of reality

Catching them completely off guard with her notion

Everyone is expecting her to explode or flat out fold

But she holds her position

Sticking to her guns she bares her soul

By saying nothing more than **K**eep **I**t **M**oving.

Sankofa
"Return and Get It"

Part IV: Lessons Learned

I have learned that no matter how much I mature I will still make mistakes. No matter how many times I practice and prepare I know sometimes I will still fail. No matter how many times he breaks my heart I understand that I will love again. The difference between yesterday and today is that today I know I will be ok.

~Let the butterflies go~
Veronica Patrice

~~2005-2008

You have already heard the good, bad and some ugly but shit still happens. No matter how far you believe you have come something will still test you. I have experienced and seen so much I should really be an expert but trust I am not. I still fall victim to certain things and haters definitely still exist but today they do not stress me. I dedicate this final chapter to my ladies still in the struggle. Love, Peace and Success!!

The Writing on the Wall

What if I never left

I wonder what life would be like without him

What if we were never introduced

After five years could I still be in love with him

The writing on the wall draws a picture of me and him

I believe life with him would be beautiful

I can't picture my life without some piece of him

Even as a friend I would consider him irreplaceable

What if he never met her

I wonder would we still be together

What if he would have married her

Would his love for me still be there

The writing on the wall does not show her

Everything happens for a reason

So there's no need to question her

It is what it is but hopefully our journey has just begun

Veronica Patrice

What if I never left him

I wonder how things would be if I would have had his baby

What if I would have married him

Would our love just have faded

The writing on the wall proves that he didn't deserve me

Babies come from love and love no longer lived here

We had no foundation besides he didn't know how to keep me

But me and you had true love and somehow it's always there

What if I didn't forgive you

I wonder if she didn't cheat would you still look for me

What if she kept the baby could I still talk to you

Or would our love just have been a forgotten memory

The writing on the wall wouldn't let me hate you

Though I wanted to and probably should have I didn't

Honestly I didn't wait for you but I never forgot you

I no longer question destiny because it was already written.

All 4 One

As I lay my mind starts replaying all I've done

I lied, cheated and stole; all for him that is

I lied to my friends to be with that one

I cheated my family out of time by becoming his

Once upon a time I carried weight for the team

Even though I was the only player I risked it all for him

But he never had my back I guess it was all a dream

Because for him I would and for me he didn't

I got caught up in the glam I saw what I wanted to see

I saw a man hustling and grinding for me

He was grinding and hustling alright

He was fucking me crazy and I gave him all of me

I got fat from the cake but I now have diabetic ways

Yeah he kept me laced with the finest

And I did love him but it was a wrap after the chase

He wanted what he couldn't have but now I'm his

Veronica Patrice

So where did the love go; it left when I said yes

What happened to all 4 one and one 4 all

I guess my good good wasn't his best

I'm cool though; I'm going to stand up and face it all

I'll take this one on the chin as a lesson learned

Because I'll never give all of me to anyone again

I got my heart back but it was tarnished and burned

Not yet dead so I know it'll live to love again

Even still I'm going to keep everyone at a distance

Loyalty is hard to come by and honesty is even harder

Respect has become damn near nonexistent

My most cherished bond is the one between my pen and paper.

Eternally Tight

We've been cool since we were three years old

You were the first person I ran to when I had my first crush

When shit hit the fan at my house you were the only one I told

You were my accomplice/alibi and the only one I could trust

You are more than a friend to me I consider you my family

Twenty years later and we are still the best of friends

I tell you all of my crazy ideas and you actually believe in me

When you got married I thought things would be different

I thought I wouldn't see or talk to you as much

In the back of my mind I feared that we might grow apart

But in all actuality nothing really changed between us

You have always had my back even as a wife and mother

When your husband was murdered I sincerely felt your pain

I wish I could have done something besides be there

But sometimes in times like this you just need a friend

Be it good or bad we can always depend on each other

Like when I walked in on Marcus and my-so-called friend

You had my back; I beat his ass while you whopped hers

We've definitely had our share of compromising predicaments

If it wasn't a cheating boyfriend then it was the losers/haters

You know more about me than I know about myself

Even my secrets are not surprises to you

Like when I told you I was still in love with Jay you just smiled

Honestly we wouldn't be together today if it wasn't for you

You are my best friend; I truly love and cherish you

We have a bond like no other nothing or no one can break it

I'm really happy that through it all I can always count on you

And for that reason we are and always will be Eternally Tight.

Life after Death

One day you're here and the next

Well you know the rest but no one is promised tomorrow

You only get one chance to give this thing called life your best

We have to live our lives like there is no tomorrow

But at the same time we need to consider our legacy

Everything we do is a map to what we will eventually be

No one is perfect but everything we do we will reap

As the saying goes "what's done in the dark will come to light"

Closet haters better watch out you may be able to deceive life

But death's karma has a bitter bite

I know that I've done wrong and I to am guilty of what I write

You see everyone sins but the point is to try to better our life

I'm not judging you I am merely guiding you

Because so many times people take this life for granted

You can't negotiate time so don't waste the time given to you

I use to fear death because there was so much I still required

But the truth of the matter is that decision isn't left up to me

Live life before death because no one knows what's after.

Focus

Stop but I can't

I feel trapped in my thoughts

I tried to break this trance

But he has my mind really caught

I'm caught in him

In the man I think he may be

I see the man I always wanted in him

Is he too good to be true or is he running game on me

Somehow he always says the right things

His answers are so perfect to me

Even when I think I've caught him he flips things

He really seems to just be into me

Not material things or my body but me

The questions he ask always insight me

And he actually remembers everything he's asked me

This man has me gone but I need to focus on me

I need to get back on my hustle

I'm not pushing these books hard enough

But then he comes over to cuddle

All That Glitters

Omg I can't stand him… not really though

I'm feeling him but what if this is just an act

Sure he hasn't tried anything but what if

Everything is moving so fast

We've only been talking for a few weeks

Yet I know his life story and family history

I know his political and religious stance

But for some reason I still run from destiny

Fear of the unknown stops me from giving him a chance.

M.I.A

Certain times of the day

My man for some reason comes up M.I.A

His phone is always dead so he says

But it only happens at night rarely during the day

Usually when I call he answers

But when he doesn't he acts like I'm the one trippin

Sure he has two cell phones but he still can't answer

One is dead and the other usually has no reception

I just don't understand how his phone dies on schedule

Or how he has no reception when we have Verizon

I hate to assume the unthinkable

But I can't just sit back and ignore the signs I'm seeing

Even though I've never caught him cheating

My intuition is telling me that he may be creepin

Even still he always claim that he's just grinding

But hustling is always his excuse

Why didn't you call me back; I was on the block

Why were you late, I was out grinding for you

I understand him grinding but does he not see the clock

All That Glitters

It's four in the morning and he's still not answering

If the shoes were reversed what would he do

Would he just sit around wondering

I doubt it but I don't want another dude

I want him to appreciate me before I walk out

Because I now find it hard to even trust him

So yeah I'm trippin but honestly it's his fault

He claims that he's not cheating but I don't believe him

I'm always pissed and bitching because he's M.I.A

And the last thing I wanna do is leave him

But if he don't answer this phone they'll find him D.O.A!

Questions

Is it worth the trouble?

Are we even in love?

Why aren't we a happy couple?

Why all we do is cuss and fuss?

Where did things go wrong?

Why does he disrespect me?

Why can't we get along?

Why can't we agree to disagree?

Why is everything an uphill battle?

Why can't he see things from my point of view?

Why do my feelings never matter?

Why doesn't he recognize the things that he do?

Why is he so jealous?

Why does he only try when another brotha is in the picture?

He has my heart but why is he so careless?

Why do I stay when I know I deserve better?

How can I love someone when I question their love?

What do I do when I'm fed up?

Do I stay hoping things will go back to how it was?

Or do I leave because I'm tired of him fucking up?

How do I know what's best for me?

Why doesn't he fight for me?

Why is it so easy for him to give up on me?

Why can't he just love me?

Why he is thirty years old and still not a man?

Why is he still so immature?

Why does he treat me like a groupie or a fan?

Why do I put myself through this?

Even after all of my questions I'm still questioning if it's even worth it.

Made

Everything in my life has come full circle

Touching the sky no longer seems impossible

My dreams have suddenly become so achievable

I'm now ready to tackle any battle and every obstacle

I couldn't careless about haters and nay sayers

Because I'm on a mission they cannot suspend

I welcome doubt and skepticism

Because simple minds are just that simple

I now walk with my head high

And I do so because I'm suppose to

You see me smiling and you wonder why

How can she be smiling after everything I put her through

I smile even after your resentment and deception

I was made tough you can say that I get it from my mama

I could hold grudges and seek revenge but for what reason

You're looking for flaws while I'm adding zeros and comas

I'm homegrown USDA certified I'm suppose to be here

This is my house you're just a counterfeit made in china

You should think twice before questioning if I belong here

All That Glitters

The only thing that can stop me now is dying

But with my set-up I'll be fine long after I leave here

I was once shy but I now speak with assurance and power

Ain't it funny how you assumed I would always be there

You thought turning your back would keep me stuck here

Please, I tried to warn people about betting against me

But foolish minds always seem to think alike

You may have crossed the finish line before me

But the jokes on you I was ahead of you at first sight

My life made me and your life motivated me

You talked about it and I accomplished it

You resented and wished the worst of me

But I thank you because ironically you propelled me to make it.

*******Sneak Preview*******

Read an excerpt from the highly anticipated follow-up to Veronica Patrice's Debut.

The Definition of K.A.R.M.A
A Novel

"Will the defendant please rise? You have been convicted of two counts of A-2 Felony possession of narcotics with the intent to sale, racketeering, the kidnapping and ransom attempt of a minor, drug trafficking, blackmail and tax invasion. The district attorney and the jury were both very merciful to you; coincidence or not you should thank them.

The jury thinks you are a misguided young man but believes with the right guidance you could be rehabilitated. Unlike them I come across your kind everyday. You are scum and even though it could not be proven today I know you are one of the leaders in the Javier Cartel.

I also believe you did murder those two cops as well as smuggle drugs into the United States. Even though you were initially facing life in prison I am only able to give the state maximum for the charges you were convicted for.

By the power invested in me by the state of New Jersey I hereby sentence you to no more than 15 years but no less than 8 years to be served in a maximum-security correctional facility. I also render the defendant to pay the court a total of $1.5 million dollars in restitution, which is the maximum in the state of New Jersey. Court is adjourned."

Karma remained frozen on the court bench for what seemed like hours. She was unable to hear the screams and sighs all she could hear was the judge saying no less than eight years, eight fucking years and $1.5 million dollars. Their house in Newark, their cars, their bank accounts and credit cards were all depleted. Everything she owned and even her husband was considered state property.

www.ingramcontent.com/pod-product-compliance
Lightning Source LLC
Chambersburg PA
CBHW051925240626
47153CB00004B/1369
* 9 7 8 0 6 1 5 2 5 2 4 2 1 *